THE Mermaid Daughters OF THE MOUNTAIN LAKE KINGDOM

BY S. MCCOY

The Mermaid Daughters of the Mountain Lake Kingdom
Trilogy Christian Publishers
A Wholly Owned Subsidiary of Trinity Broadcasting Network
2442 Michelle Drive
Tustin, CA 92780

For information, address Trilogy Christian Publishing
Rights Department, 2442 Michelle Drive, Tustin, Ca 92780.

For information about special discounts for bulk purchases, please contact Trilogy Christian Publishing.
Manufactured in the United States of America

10 9 8 7 6 5 4 3 2 1
Library of Congress Cataloging-in-Publication Data is available.
ISBN: 978-1-63769-714-6
ISBN: 978-1-63769-715-3

Dedication

This book is written for my two wonderful sons. They are my greatest pride and joy and the two most amazing blessings in my life.

Acknowledgments

First and foremost, I give a big thank you to Sarah for her encouragement with all my artistic endeavors. Additionally, I thank Mermaid Linden for introducing me to the modern mermaid world full of wonder and possibilities. Finally, I would like to acknowledge the late great C.S. Lewis for his masterful style of writing. His creative writing style has served as a powerful inspiration for me with his unique use of allegories within fictional environments that have produced countless literary masterpieces that all ages can enjoy…

Introduction

My hope in writing this book was to create a fun and entertaining family fairytale, featuring mermaid twin daughters and their loving father in order to tell a story of unconditional love, forgiveness, and restoration. I chose the well-known background of the majestic and rugged California Eastern Sierra Mountains with their crystal-blue lakes as the location to tell the story and I set the time of the story during the "Wild West" era of California's early "Gold Rush."

I would like to greatly thank you for your consideration in choosing to spend time reading my book, and I hope you are entertained, immersed, and hopefully inspired! Now please enjoy *The Mermaid Daughters of The Mountain Lake Kingdom*!

S. McCoy

Chapter 1

Once upon a time, there was a very honorable and just Merman King named George. His Kingdom was very far away from humans in a beautiful, majestic mountain lake that is towered by a magnificent mountain peak made of sparkling crystal. The King's lake overlooked a wonderful forest, full of tall green pine trees, breathtaking giant granite rocks, and rushing mountain rivers that connected to many other smaller crystal-blue lakes. These crystal-blue lakes were inhabited by all different kinds of interesting and colorful mountain fish, like rainbow trout, redeye bass, and pink salmon. The surrounding lake's forests were full of charming wildlife, little fuzzy tailed chipmunks, swift foxes, and strong and courageous bears. The clean and crisp mountain skies over the lakes were populated with vibrant multicolored birds such as blue jays, redheaded woodpeckers, and mighty eagles. All the living creatures in the Mountain Lake Kingdom respected and admired King George, because of his fairness, kindness, and justice as their King. George had two very smart and beautiful twin mermaid daughters that he loved and adored named Mary and Mamie. His daughters were the apple of his eye and they brought him great joy, and they all lived very happily together in this majestic mountain paradise until one day…

As the 21st first birthday approached for Mary and Mamie they became very excited with anticipation, because mermaid tradition is on your 21st birthday the King would give his offspring a portion of their inheritance so they could start establishing their own kingdoms. Mary, who was the older of the twins (by just one minute) was excited to follow in her father's footsteps and hoped her inheritance would be one of the crystal-blue lakes that were connected to the King's Lake by the rushing mountain rivers. She dreamed that one day she could be Queen of her own small lake kingdom, because like her father, Mary greatly enjoyed looking after and caring for the animals in her father's Kingdom. Mamie on the other hand, was more interested in a portion of the royal treasure that was secretly hidden in the deep waters of the King's Lake. Mamie loved the beautiful jewelry that was part of the King's Royal Treasure, and it was made up of sparkling diamonds, rosy-red rubies, and deep blue sapphires that made spectacular rings, bracelets, and necklaces. Mamie would go there without the King's permission sometimes and try on the jewelry and dream of the day that this jewelry would be all hers. However, she did not care as much for the many pieces of large gold that were in the King's treasure because she could not wear the gold pieces, so she thought to herself that one day that portion could just go to her sister Mary. That way she could have all the beautiful jewelry for herself someday.

After waiting what seemed to be a very long time for the mermaid twins, their 21st birthdays finally arrived. They were so excited to see what their father would give them. There was a big celebration, and all the water, air, and land animals of the kingdom were invited. Everyone had a great time and enjoyed themselves at the twin's birthday celebration. Afterwards, George told Mary what her portion of her inheritance would be. She was given the big crystal-blue lake that was right next to the King's Lake, and he ordered the lake be called "Lake Mary." Mary was so happy and excited that her dreams had come true, and she would be Queen of her own lake kingdom! Additionally, this lake was connected to her father's lake by a beautiful rushing river so she could come and go quickly and easily to her father's magnificent crystal-blue lake right next to hers.

Next, it was time for Mamie to receive her portion of her inheritance from her father. She was so eager to hear, and she desperately wanted some of the royal treasure so she could finally wear the beautiful jewelry for everyone to see. However, to Mamie's surprise, the King gave her a beautiful crystal-blue lake that was right next to "Lake Mary," and this lake was also connected by a rushing mountain river, and he ordered it named "Lake Mamie." Mamie was disappointed and was so sad she did not receive the royal jewelry she wanted. So, she boldly asked her father if she could have the royal jewelry instead of the lake. Her father was taken back by her request a bit at first, then he thought about her request for a minute. Shortly after George told his daughter he loved her but said no to her request for the royal jewelry. He told Mamie, that portion of her inheritance would be for another time in the future.

Mamie pleaded with her father and said, "But Daddy, my lake is much smaller than Mary's, and this is unfair!"

George replied calmly and lovingly, "Mamie, but your lake is very special! It has the underground river that the new fish swim up, so you get to see all the new members of the Mountain Lake Kingdom and greet them as they arrive at their new home. However, Mamie it is very important to remember that the underground river leads to 'The Great Barrier Chasm' that mermaids are forbidden to cross. If any mermaid crosses it, they will lose their ability to swim back the same way and will have entered the domain of the Human Kingdom!"

Then, Mamie realizing she could not change her father's mind, she slowly nodded in agreement but was still very disappointed. However, she was a little happy at least her lake had something special that Mary's did not have. Then she slowly swam away still a little sad, but now interested in investigating her new lake more closely.

Chapter 2

In the meantime, far across the mountains in the Human Kingdom and locked in a jail cell in a town called Carson, was a sneaking convict named Slick, who had recently been arrested for bank robbery. Slick was a tall, very thin, and handsome man with slicked-back black hair, and he had sneaky shady eyes. Slick was also very smart; unfortunately, he did not use his intelligence for good things. On the contrary, he spent most of his time planning and scheming new ways to steal money and gold from good innocent folks. He had a partner in crime with who he currently shared a jail cell, and his name was Derby.

Derby was a short and stocky man who wore a brown derby to make himself look taller. He ran away from home at an early age, and he never practiced the good hygiene that his parents tried to teach him. Therefore, he was always a little stinky and often times, had flies buzzing around him from not taking a bath. He also never took good care of his teeth, so now he was missing a few. Derby dropped out of school at an early age, and he admired Slick because he thought Slick was very smart and he liked his devious mind.

Slick was whispering his latest scheme to Derby so the guard could not hear his plans. He told Derby about a story he had heard from his cousin Jimbo, who works in a nearby goldmine. This story was about a secret lake on the other side of the mountains. This secret lake had a sparkling crystal peak behind it and hidden in the lake was outlaw gold. Slick went on to say, a few years ago some outlaws were on the run after robbing a gold-filled train, and they had to quickly hide their stolen gold, and leave it behind because they were being chased by The Revered Federal Marshall McCoy. Legend has it, that this lake was surrounded by fierce wild animals and the treasure was being guarded in the lake by creatures that were half-man and half-fish. Derby, after hearing the story seemed to be confused and a little scared about the fierce wild animals and lake creatures, so he asked Slick how he planned on getting that gold since that was a secret lake over the mountains, and they were both currently locked up in jail.

Slick told him the plan, "We will wait until midnight tonight when the moon is full. Then, my cousin Jimbo will come to this jail and break us out!"

Derby asked, "How's he going to do that Slick?"

Slick went on to tell him, "Jimbo is very big, strong, and full of muscles from working in the goldmines, and he can bend these window bars with his bare hands quietly, so the guards won't hear. Jimbo is bringing a horse-drawn wagon full of hay, we will hide underneath the hay until we're far out of Carson. Then we will ride day and night through the old miner's mountain passes until we find that secret lake full of gold."

"What about the fierce wild animals and the half-man and half-fish that are guarding the gold treasure?" Derby asked as his voice begin to shake.

Slick replied "Jimbo is bringing torches and dynamite that he stole from the goldmine. We will use the torches to scare away the fierce wild animals and bring the dynamite in case we have any trouble getting to the treasure."

"Wow, you're so smart Slick," Derby said, "but I think you forgot about one thing, 'The Revered Marshall McCoy!' I'm sure they will send him after us."

Slick replied, “Don’t you worry about him, I have a special trap planned for him,” as Slick belted out an evil laugh and a devious smile crept over his face.

Chapter 3

Meanwhile back at the beautiful crystal-blue mountain lakes, a few days had passed since the twin's birthday celebration. Mary and Mamie were enjoying their new lakes and were spending time meeting all the fish that lived in them. The King had a new request that day for the twins, that a census be taken in "Lake Mary" and "Lake Mamie" to determine how many fish lived in each lake. Mary went right to work, she always respected her father's requests and always tried to do her best job because she loved and admired him greatly. Mamie on the other hand was not always so eager to listen to her father's requests and often times questioned him on why she had to do particular tasks. Even though she loved and admired her father, she often thought she knew what was best.

So, instead of taking the census of her lake like her father had requested her to do, she spent the day swimming and lounging around the lake and listening to local fish gossip. She also went swimming near the underground river that led to "The Great Barrier Chasm" and was listening to the fish stories from the newly arriving fish families that were swimming up from the underground river. There was one fish story that was particularly interesting to Mamie. It was about the shining gold objects that the fish said they had seen in the lake in the Human Kingdom just before they swam up the underground river. Mamie asked the fish if the shiny objects looked like jewelry. They replied yes, the fish said they looked like dangly gold earrings or a necklace with charms. This was very intriguing to Mamie because she still did not have any gold jewelry from the Kings Royal Treasure, and as the day went on, she became more and more curious about the underground river, and the lake in the Human Kingdom full of jewelry and thought perhaps there was more and different kinds of treasure in that lake.

At the end of the day before nightfall, Mary swam to the King's Lake and gave the King her census report of the number of fish in "Lake Mary," but Mamie never arrived at the King's Lake to give her report. The King was concerned for Mamie and asked Mary if she would swim down to "Lake Mamie" and check on her sister and retrieve the census and then report back to him. She agreed and then quickly swam off to find her sister.

CHAPTER 3

After swimming to "Lake Mamie," she found her sister lounging around the edge of the lake and Mamie told her that she had not had time to complete the census and was not sure when she would have time to do it. Mary told Mamie she had already completed her census and there should have been plenty of time to complete her report as well because her lake was even smaller and less populated than Mary's.

This made Mamie upset and a little jealous of Mary's bigger lake, so she snapped at her, "You are such a goodie, goodie, single-fin! You always do just what father asks without ever thinking for yourself. Why should we have to report our census to him anyway? It's just unnecessary busy work for us! You know Mary, father is not telling us the whole story about that underground river and the lake in the Human Kingdom. I heard it's full of shiny gold jewelry and treasure."

Then Mary responded, "You know that's not true! Who did you hear that nonsense from anyways?"

Mamie fired back, "I heard it from the fish families that swam up the underground river from the lake in the Human Kingdom!"

"Oh, Mamie," Mary said, "That is just a fish story! Sometimes those fish like to exaggerate their stories and gossip about things that are not true. That shiny jewelry is probably just fish lures and fish traps they are seeing. Besides, that has nothing to do with us anyway. That's the Human Kingdom down there and that stuff belongs to them and is dangerous!"

Mamie thought about what Mary had said then she replied, "Maybe, but maybe there is beautiful jewelry down in that lake. I think we should swim down the underground river and see for ourselves, and if it is a real jewelry, we can have it for our own lake kingdoms."

"Oh no!" Mary replied. "You know what father told us about the underground river. We must never, never go down it! It is for the fish only and it leads to 'The Great Barrier Chasm,' and if a mermaid cross over it, we will not be able to swim back the same way!"

Then Mamie said, "Well then how come the fish can swim up the river then, and we can't?"

Mary replied, "You know what father said, there is only a small rock tunnel that fish can fit through, but mermaids are way too big to pass through it. You need to stop thinking about that stuff and please just get back to completing your census as father asked."

Mamie paused for a moment, then said "Okay, tell father I'll have his precious census for him tomorrow." Then she swam away to be alone and to pout a bit.

In the Meantime, Slick and Derby had successfully escaped the jail cell as planned with the help of Jimbo and were several days away from Carson now. They were riding on the old mining trails heading towards the mountain lakes. However, they were not exactly sure where the secret mountain lake with the outlaw gold was. Jimbo was driving the horse-drawn wagon and knew the mining trails very well. Jimbo is a big and tall man with a big unshaven scruffy black-beard and wore an old beaten-up miner's hat with old tore-up overalls. Jimbo had been in and out of jail several times mostly for stealing, and unfortunately every time he got out of jail it never seemed to take him too long before he got himself back into trouble again with the law.

Jimbo just had a general idea of the mountain lake area from the story he had heard about in the goldmine, and they were heading in that general direction. However, the trio was getting tired from riding day and night after escaping from the jail. Then, Slick had an idea; he knew of a lake nearby and close to the mountains that were used now and then by outlaws like them that were hiding from the law. It was surrounded by steep mountain rocks and forests, and it had only one way in and one way out, so they would not be surprised by a local sheriff posse. The best part was this lake was connected to another lake by an underground river and it had plenty of fish that they could catch and eat. So, the three convicts decided to go hideout there for a while, until they could figure out where the secret mountain lake full of outlaw gold was located.

As expected, The Revered Federal Marshall McCoy was summoned to Carson to find the escaped convicts. Marshall McCoy is a tall and handsome man with dark hair, and he wore a big black cowboy hat. He is a great experienced investigator with keen senses and these abilities he uses to track down escaped convicts. He patrols "The Great Wild West" on a big strong Palomino horse he called Buddy, and he mostly works tracking down the worst of the worst outlaws and escaped convicts. He is greatly feared by those outlaws and convicts because he is like a bloodhound, that slowly tracks down those outlaws and convicts and eventually, he always finds them and brings them to justice.

On this day, he started his investigation at the jail cell and quickly determined the two convicts had escaped by a horse-drawn wagon with the help of a third man with size 15 boots. He knew this because of the big footprint he left outside of the jail cell. The horse-drawn wagon had two horses and was quite heavy, probably loaded with supplies, the three men, and most likely dynamite. He knew the wagon was heavily loaded due to the deep wheel-marks the wagon wheels left behind and the wagon was heading southwest towards the mining trails. He knew those old mining trails very well because it always seemed that the convicts had a thirst for gold and were usually trying to steal it from good hardworking folks and goldmines. He called for his horse Buddy, and the two rode off following the trail of the convicts.

Slick and his gang finally arrived at the old hideout lake where they could lay-low and hide from the law until they could figure out where the secret lake full of gold was located. They unpacked their things and built a small campfire out of wood from the forest and placed their sleeping bags around the campfire. They decided to wait until the morning to go fishing, so they could fish next to the underground river and catch as many fish as they could. So, without fish to eat that night, Derby made another portion of his famous bean soup that the trio had been eating exclusively for the last several days. As expected, the convicts again had another explosive and somewhat stinky night sitting around the campfire planning and scheming their next move.

Slick asked Jimbo if he had any idea how close the secret lake might be. Jimbo, seem to think they were close to it, probably somewhere further up the mountain as there were many lakes nearby and they were all connected by mountain rivers. He knew that because the fish always swim up the rivers to the upper lakes to lay their eggs. Then Slick asked Jimbo, "Where do you suppose this underground river from this lake goes to?"

Jimbo replied, "I don't know, nobody could know."

Slick leaned back, pushed his hat back, and scratched his head to think then said, "Very interesting, if nobody knows where it goes, I think that would be a good spot to hide tressure, if I had some to hide, don't you think Jimbo?"

Derby, chimed in, "Yep! that would be a great place Slick for sure! If we only knew where that lake is that underground river went to… I bet yah, those fish know where it is Slick! Now if only those fish could talk!"

Jimbo shot back, "Yeah Da-Da-Deeerby, if only those fish could talk..." Then Slick and Jimbo, broke-out in laughter at what Derby had said. Derby was a little embarrassed realizing what he had said didn't sound so smart, so he pulled his hat down tight because he was upset, and then went back to eating more bean soup alone.

Chapter 5

Meanwhile early the next morning before the fish were awake, Mamie was becoming more and more curious about the gold jewelry in the lake and the underground river. She thought to herself, that maybe her father was wrong about the fish tunnel and Mary was wrong about the jewelry being just fish lures and fish traps. Finally, curiosity got the best of her, and she swam up to the entrance of the underground river and looked in the rocks as far as she could down the river, and she could not see any danger. It looked like a big water cave to her, and she did not understand how this could be dangerous. So, she swam back and forth in front of the cave entrance and was thinking to herself. She thought, what could be the harm with just swimming a little way in the cave to check it out, and if it got too dangerous, she would just simply turn around and head back. After a few more nervous laps back and forth in front of the entrance, she decided to go for it and started slowly swimming down the underground river.

At first, there were no problems at all, and the water seemed very calm and peaceful, so she swam a little further down the tunnel. It was getting darker and darker as she went further down the river, and it seemed like the water was getting faster. She still did not see any danger and decided to keep swimming further down the river. However, what she could not see because it was dark was the walls around the river were getting closer and surrounded her like a funnel. Mamie started to get a little nervous as the water seem to be really picking up speed. She thought, I will go just a little bit further, I want to see for myself what "The Great Barrier Chasm" looks like.

All of a sudden, she could feel the walls of the river surrounding her and the water was rushing as if pulling her down faster, and faster. She tried to turn around, but the walls were too narrow now, and she could not turn around. Then, she started to panic because the water was going too fast and the current too strong and she could not stop. Just then she saw it! Straight ahead of her was a great chasm and she was heading right towards it. It was too late there was nothing she could do, so she put her head down and swam straight at it as hard as she could! Then she was shot out of the river tunnel like a canon and flew over "The Great Barrier Chasm," and unto the other side and she splashed down safely into a wide slow running underground river that then slowly carried her down through a cave opening and into a new unfamiliar lake.

It was just breaking dawn, as Mamie swam into the new unfamiliar lake, and she wondered if this was the lake in the Human Kingdom that the fish talked about. She was very unsure of her surroundings, so she swam very cautiously staying below water as not to be seen. Mamie was scared and started to cry a little, she realized what her father had said about "The Great Barrier Chasm" was true, and there was no way she could go back that way, the chasm was too big. She thought, *how could I ever get back home?* And home felt so far away from where she was. This made her even more sad, and the tears rolled down her face uncontrollably.

Then she thought maybe there was another way out of this lake and another way home. So, she wiped the tears from her eyes and started to investigate the lake looking for another exit. She swam around the edges of the lake for what seemed a very long time, but unfortunately there did not seem to be another way out, and even worse was the lake was not full of gold jewelry like the fish had said. She was very disappointed and because she had no success underwater, she tried looking on the surface. As she slowly peaked up through the water, she could make out images of two men standing on the edge of the lake. One man was very big and looked like a giant to her and the other one tall and skinny. They were both wearing hats and had wooden tree branches in their hands with a string attached that was running into the water. Mamie was curious about where the strings led to, so she went back underwater for a closer look.

As she slowly approached the string, she could see a small shiny coin attacked to the end of it. She quickly reached out to grab it, and then she felt a sharp poke on her hand! She pulled her hand back and noticed there was a metal hook stuck in her hand. Even though it hurt, she quickly pulled the hook out of her hand and swiftly swim away from the string and the coin. She thought to herself, that was a fish lure and a fish trap just like Mary had said. This made her sad again because she realized she lost her own lake kingdom to come here and find nothing but untrue fish stories and fool's gold. She decided to swim further around the lake until she had completely circled it. The lake was very deep and there was no other way out, except the underground river that only fish could swim through. She felt very discouraged, and her situation seemed hopeless.

As evening approached and the sun was setting over the King's Lake, Mary was back talking to her father, and they were both waiting for Mamie to arrive back with her census report. As they continued to wait the King became concerned as to why Mamie had not returned with her report. He requested Mary go again to "Lake Mamie" to retrieve her sister, so she swiftly swam off to find Mamie. She searched and searched the lake but was unable to find her.

She asked many of the fish that lived there if they had seen Mamie today, and they all replied, "No, and they had not seen her at all today."

Mary became very concerned that something had happened to her, and she hoped that Mamie had not swam down the underground river that she kept talking about. So, she immediately swam back to the King's Lake and told her father she could not find her and told him she was worried her sister may have swam down the underground river that she was talking about yesterday.

The King was now very, very concerned and summoned all the lake creatures, the land animals, and the birds of the air that lived in his Kingdom. He requested that they search high and low and every square inch of his Kingdom and report back to him if they see Mamie, and they all did immediately what the king had requested. After a furious search of the Kingdom throughout the night, all the animals sadly reported back to the King his daughter was nowhere to be found. At the news, the King was so sad and heartbroken, and tears started to roll down his face, because he knew what Mary had feared was probably true, that Mamie had gone down the underground river and crossed "The Great Barrier Chasm."

The King summoned the strongest, most honorable, and most trustworthy Eagle in his Kingdom, and at his word, this mighty magnificent Eagle approached the King. The King requested him to go on a special mission for the Kingdom. He asked the mighty magnificent Eagle to leave the Mountain Kingdom and fly to the Human Kingdom, to the lake of human outlaws and fool's gold, the lake that had only one way out through the forest trail! He then requested the Eagle find his lost daughter who he greatly loved and lead her home through the only land exit that was still available, the forest trail. The mighty magnificent Eagle nodded proudly in agreement to the King's request and immediately took flight to find Mamie and complete his mission for the King.

Chapter 7

Meanwhile the next day, Marshall McCoy was getting closer and was hot on the trail of the convicts and the secret lake. He usually worked alone, but this time he thought it would be wise to get help locating the escaped convicts from an old friend that lived nearby, who was very familiar with this area's mountain trails and the surrounding crystal-blue lakes. So, he pulled off the trail of the convicts and started following a big beautiful fast-moving mountain river for a few miles which eventually led to a majestic and massive waterfall. On the other side of the waterfall just down the river, was his old friend Braveman.

Braveman was from a great and noble indigenous tribe of Native American's that inhabited the valley lands near the mountain passes, and not only was Braveman Marshall McCoy's good friend, he also was the Chief's son. He was very tall and strong, and he had long black flowing hair and he was in charge of security for his tribe. He received his name from his father the tribal Chief because of his great bravery and strength. He rode a beautiful multicolor Paint horse with big brown and white spots, and he called his horse Bear. He had known Marshall McCoy for a longtime and he also knew he was a good and noble man who kept his word. Therefore, and on occasion when trouble making outlaws would pass through the tribal areas, he would help him bring those troublemakers to justice and by doing this also ensuring his tribe would remain safe from the outlaw's schemes.

Braveman was very happy to see his friend, and it had been a long time since he had seen him last. He invited him to stay for a meal and had his horse Buddy attended to with cold water and fresh hay. Over the special prepared warm meal, Marshall McCoy explained to him about Slick and his gang of convicts he was tracking. He went on to explain, about the wagon full of dynamite that the gang was riding in, and about the strongman that bent the bars of the jail cell to free Slick and Derby. He warned him that he thought these men were very dangerous and asked him if he would help locate these convicts. Braveman immediately agreed to help find them.

After, he went on to tell Marshall McCoy about a report from one of his scouts that had followed some deep wagon wheel tracks to a secret lake in the mountains near them. The scout did not follow them to the lake because there is only one way in and one way out and he did not want to be detected. The scout went on to say there was smoke from a campfire and he thought there may be a few outlaws in their group, so the scout headed back here to warn the tribe.

Marshall McCoy quickly jumped up and said, "I am sure that's them! The deep wagon wheels tracks are the same ones that I have been following, will your scout take me to that secret mountain lake?" Braveman agreed and additionally he decided to bring twelve of his best and strongest warriors with them to make sure they brought these dangerous convicts to justice.

Chapter 8

In the meantime, at the secret outlaw lake, as sunset was approaching and the convicts were around the campfire, Slick and Jimbo were busy teasing Derby because he stunk so bad and that there were flies around him again. Derby thought to himself, when was the last time he had taken a bath and then he realized it had been several weeks. So, to stop the teasing from Slick and Jimbo, he decided to go take a quick dip in the lake to rinse off.

At the same time just before dusk, Mamie had just finished swimming around the lake in hopes of finding another water exit, but she had no success. She decided to take a break on a rock close to shore and stretch out for a little nap because she was exhausted from the day's events.

When she did, she suddenly noticed some leaves rustling on the shore behind the trees and thought maybe it was one of her land animal friends, so she looked on hopefully. However, and much to her surprise it was not an animal, it was a human! She had never seen a human up close before, but she knew what they looked like from the fish descriptions. They had two legs and stood upright and primarily stayed on land, like the two men she had seen earlier with the fishing lure. Her father had warned her not to talk to humans, but to hide from them. So, she quickly hopped off her rock and into the water to hide and then peaked out at the human from behind the rock.

Derby had heard a big splash and thought wow! That must have been a big fish jumping out of the water. The big splash startled him a little bit and he thought twice about going in the lake for a bath when it was getting dark. So, he just decided to sit on the lakeshore and put his feet in the water instead. He started taking off his boots when he saw what he thought was a woman peeking out from behind the rocks and staring at him.

He called out to the woman, “Hey there! Who are you?”

Mamie, realizing she had been seen and was scared so she went further behind the rock. She started thinking to herself, that maybe this human could help her get home. Besides, he looked much smaller than the other human men she had seen earlier, and he really did not look dangerous.

Again, he called out to her, and this time Mamie came

out from behind the rock and replied, “I’m Mamie, what’s your name?”

He said, “People just call me Derby. What are you doing here, out in the middle of nowhere?”

She thought then replied, “I am lost and far away from my home, would you be able to help get me back to my home?”

Derby pulled his hat off and scratched his head as if deep in thought and said “Slick won’t let me help no one, I mean, I can’t help you right now! We are about ready to pull off an important job. I mean, I’m working, and I don’t have time to help no one.”

She was sad and replied, “Okay.” and then slowly started to swim off.

He called out to her again as she was swimming away, “Where’s your home anyways?”

She stopped swimming and turned around and swam closer towards Derby again and thought she would ask him for help one more time. Then she started telling him about her home, the Mountain Lake Kingdom, and about her father. He looked confused and asked her what she meant by the Mountain Lake Kingdom.

She said, "Derby, I'm a mermaid and I have my own lake now."

Still confused he replied, "Wait, what's a mermaid, anyways?"

She thought for a moment then said, "Mermaids have a single fin and no legs, and we live in the water, See!" Then she splashed him with water as she showed him her mermaid tail.

He jumped back from the shore shocked and then he started rubbing his eyes as he could not believe what he was seeing. Now he was more confused, and he did not know what to do, but he thought Slick would know.

He said "Wait here for a minute, I need to go get my gang! I mean my friends. I think maybe they'll want to go to that mermaid kingdom. I mean, I think they'll help you get home. Just stay here a minute, I'll be right back."

She nodded in agreement and then Derby ran off to get his gang.

Derby ran back to the campfire out of breath, and he was so out of breath he could not talk at first!

Jimbo shouted, “Hey Derby you forgot your boots!” and he started laughing.

Derby finally caught his breath and was able to talk, then he started trying to explain what he had seen and what Mamie had told him.

Jimbo, started laughing at him again and said, “A talking fish? Derby, you lost your mind and have gone crazy!” Then he started laughing at Derby even harder.

Slick jumped in, “Wait a minute Jimbo, Derby did you say this fish was half-woman half-fish?”

He replied, “Yep! That’s what I said Slick. She said she was a mer, a mer, a mer-something or other,”

Slick replied, “Do you mean mermaid?”

“Yep, that’s it Slick, mermaid! She a real-life mermaid and her father has a Mountain Lake Kingdom she said!”

“Lake Kingdom? Derby, I think you did it! You stumbled unto away for us to find out where that outlaw treasure is and the secret lake! Remember how the story goes, the outlaw treasure is in a lake surrounded by fierce wild animals and protected in the water by half-fish and half-men?”

“Yeah Slick, I do, but this here is a half-woman and half-fish I said.”

Slick called Derby over to him closer with his finger and asked him for his hat, so Derby gave it to him, then Slick hit him over the head with his hat.

Then he said to him, “Her father, Derby! Her father! That’s the lake where the outlaw treasure is you knuckle-head! Take me to the mermaid, I got a plan.”

So, the trio grabbed a torch to light their way and ran off to the lakeside to find Mamie.

CHAPTER 9

They found her on the lakeshore stretched out and waiting for Derby to return, Slick and Jimbo looked shocked at first, because they had never seen a mermaid before and had only heard stories from sailors about what they looked like. Slick talked to her about her home lake and where it was located, he also asked about her father's Kingdom. Thinking Slick was a friend and was trying to help her, she told him everything about the Mountain Lake Kingdom, the many lakes, the crystal peak, and her father. She also said she was not sure how to get there from where they were currently, but once she found the lake that looked like a horseshoe, she could get home from there because that lake was very close to her own lake. Slick took it all in and he was now convinced that Mamie could lead the gang to the outlaw treasure, once they found the lake shaped like a horseshoe.

Slick told her that he and his friends would like to help her get home, but they were only poor goldminers, and they could not afford to leave the mine to take her home because he was afraid if they left the mine that outlaws would come and steal from it.

Mamie thought for a moment then she told him, "My father has a great royal treasure full of gold and he would gladly give you some for your trouble for returning me back home."

He replied, "Treasure you say! Gold treasure?"

"Yes! there is plenty, and he would be happy to give you some if you can just take me back home, please," she said.

Slick replied, "Okay, I guess we can spare the time and leave our goldmine for a little bit to help out a friend, if we're able to get paid for our trouble. We can leave first thing in the morning and try and find that horseshoe-shaped lake."

She was thrilled that he had agreed to help take her back home and she immediately swam off to find a bed for the night, so she would be well rested and be ready to travel first thing in the morning! However, she was little worried that once she got home that her father would be mad at her for breaking the mermaid rules by swimming down the underground river and leaving the Mountain Lake Kingdom and her inheritance behind. She was also a little concerned that her father may not welcome her back home, or even worse, maybe he may not want her to come back home at all.

Chapter 10

As morning broke, the mighty majestic Eagle was still desperately searching for Mamie and had flown over many lakes throughout the mountain area searching for the lake with only one forest trail in and out. As he continued to search, he finally found it and he followed the forest trail to the lake. He spotted her on the rock bed asleep close to the shore. He immediately flew down next to Mamie, and he woke her up. She was so happy to see him! She asked if her father is upset with her for leaving and she asked if her father would ever take her back into his Kingdom after she had broken the mermaid rules. The Eagle explained to her that her father loved her very much and was very sad that she was missing and wanted her back home. He had sent him to find her and lead her back home and he was not mad at her at all. She was so happy hearing that she was still loved, wanted, and forgiven!

Then she went on to tell the mighty Eagle that she had friends that were going to help get her home, if he would just lead the way. The mighty Eagle agreed because that was his orders from the King, but he warned her that the King told them they were not to have contact with the humans, and certainly not to talk with them about the Mountain Lake Kingdom. He told Mamie, he would take them into the Kingdom to the lake shaped like a horseshoe where they would be safe, but her and her friends would need to stay there until he got new instruction from the King. He also told her that it is very important that she not alert her new friends to his presence, and to make sure she carefully watched him as he led the way home, and she happily agreed.

Marshall McCoy and Braveman, with his warriors, arrived at the one way in and one way out forest trail around daybreak. The scout that had followed the wagon wheel tracks told Braveman and Marshall McCoy they had arrived at the spot where he stopped tracking the wagon and he said that he went no further. He pointed to the location where he had seen the campfire smoke just over the ridge, but there was no smoke now and additional no new wagon wheel tracks that were exiting from the forest trail yet.

After listening to what the scout had said, Marshall McCoy told his posse that they had arrived just in time, and this must be a travel day for the convicts leaving the lake on their way to their next heist. He thought the posse and their horses should hide behind the trees and wait for the convicts to pass by, and then they would surprise them and catch them off guard so they would not have time to do anything bad with the loaded wagon full of dynamite. Braveman agreed and instructed his warriors to hide behind the trees and to wait for him to give the whistle signal before they were to come out and help capture the convicts, and they all did as instructed and patiently waited for the right moment to make their move.

Meanwhile, Slick and his gang had the horse-drawn wagon loaded up and they were on the move towards the forest trail exit. Mamie was in the back of the wagon riding next to Derby. She was lying down on top of the hay, and she had a blanket over her fin as not to be noticed by other humans. From where she was laying, she could clearly see the mighty Eagle up in the sky leading the way home. Slick's gang had no idea that the Eagle was directing her, and the group had no idea of the posse hiding behind the trees just ahead. As they approached the narrow part of the trail where the posse was hiding, the Eagle let out a large screech in mid-flight, as if warning something was about to unfold.

Marshall McCoy and Braveman were hiding close together behind the trees and heard the Eagle screech and could now see Slick and his gang approaching in the horse-drawn wagon. Marshall McCoy had his hand up ready to signal to Braveman to send the whistle signal to the warriors. As the wagon came closer, he could see Derby in the back of the wagon and he knew he had all three convicts together now and he was about to lower his hand to give the signal, when he suddenly noticed a fourth person in the wagon. However, much to his surprise the person was a woman riding in the back of the wagon and she was laying down partially covered with a blanket draped over her legs.

He thought they must have captured the woman, and he became very concerned for her safety. He thought if he and the posse charged down right now and captured the convicts, the woman may be harmed. So, he called off the surprise arrest and waited for the horse-drawn wagon and the gang to pass-by and continue down the forest trail. Braveman, the warriors, and Marshall McCoy followed the wagon far enough behind as not to be seen, but close enough so if the men left the wagon, they could then rush in and rescue the woman from the convicts and after, make the arrests.

Chapter 11

After a long day of riding, Slick's gang with Mamie still in the back and the mighty Eagle leading the way arrived at the lake that looked like a horseshoe. Marshall McCoy, Braveman, and the warriors took positions behind the gang up behind the tree line and just out of sight. They were still unnoticed by the gang, and they continued to wait for just the right moment to rush down and recuse the woman. The Eagle, seeing Mamie, was now in the Kingdom and was safe for the time being at the lake shaped like a horseshoe landed in a huge pine tree to keep an eye on her and her new so-called friends.

Now that they had arrived at the lake shaped like a horseshoe, Slick and his gang were very anxious to get their hands on the gold and get out of there before sundown. That way the fierce wild animals and the half-man and half-fish creatures would not be alerted to their intentions. Then, Slick started to question Mamie about the location of the King's Lake and where exactly the gold treasure was located in the lake, and he reminded her she had promised to give him some of the royal gold treasure because they brought her back home. She explained to Slick the King's Lake was just through the forest and over the ridge. However, she told Slick she could not tell him the location of the royal gold treasure because that was a mermaid secret that she was forbidden to share This made Slick angry and he accused Mamie of breaking her promise, but Mamie had never promised Slick she would tell him the location of the royal gold treasure only that her father would give them some of the gold for returning her home to the Kingdom.

Slick got angry with her and said, "Okay, if you won't tell us then, we want all that royal gold tressure now, or we won't take you back home to the King's Lake at all. We will just keep you with us instead!"

Mamie still refused to tell Slick, so, he ordered Jimbo, "Tie her up to this wagon, so she can't escape!" Then Jimbo tied Mamie to the wagon bench as she screamed for help!

Derby asked, "Slick, what are you doing? I don't want to hurt nobody. Just let her go and will go find the gold without her help. We know where that secret lake is now, we don't need her anyway."

Slick snapped back at Derby, "Be quiet! We're not hurting her anyway! We're just making sure she can't escape! I have a plan to ransom her for all that treasure! Derby light those torches we need to set some campfires around the wagon now to scare off any fierce wild animals. I want to find her father, so we can ransom her for all that treasure!"

The mighty Eagle seeing Mamie was in trouble and those men were not her friends after all, immediately took flight to the King's Lake to inform King George and to get help to free her and bring her home safely. Once the mighty Eagle reached the King and told him he had found his daughter and she was now at the lake shaped like a horseshoe, the King was extremely happy that Mamie had been found! Then the Eagle went on to tell the King about the three human men with her and that they had tied her up and that they wanted all the royal treasure. The King quickly summoned all the animals in the Kingdom to go help capture those three human men and help Mamie escape from them. He then asked the mighty Eagle to lead the land and air animals to her location, and they all did immediately what the King requested.

Chapter 12

Meanwhile, Marshall McCoy could hear Mamie screaming for help and he saw the torches being lit. He waited until the three men moved far enough away from the wagon and started lighting the campfires around the wagon.

He turned to Braveman and said, "Now's the time! let's go rescue the woman!"

Braveman asked his men to go put out the dangerous campfires that those convicts had started while they go rescue the woman. Then he and Marshall McCoy jumped on their horse and rode towards the wagon to save Mamie and the warriors rode down to put out the fires that were quickly becoming bigger and endangering the forest.

Slick and his gang were just finishing lighting the campfires when he suddenly turned and noticed Marshall McCoy and the posse of men on horses heading right for him!

He yelled to the gang, "He found us! Quick to the wagon! Let's get out of here!" Then the trio started running to the wagon.

When they reached the horse-drawn wagon Slick said, "Wait! Don't get in!"

He noticed the twelve warriors were not heading towards them but heading towards the now raging campfires to put them out instead.

Then he said, "I have an idea! We need a distraction so we can get away!"

So, he turned and lit the back end of the wagon on fire with his torch and yelled at the horses to giddy up! This scared the two horses who were pulling the wagon, and the horses reared up on their back legs and took off running, pulling the wagon with Mamie still in it!

Then he said, "This way! They will go after the wagon and rescue the mermaid instead of chasing us!" Then the three convicts ran in a different direction away from the wagon and towards the King's Lake.

Marshall McCoy seeing that Slick had set the wagon on

fire continued to ride after the now flaming fastmoving wagon with Braveman riding next to him on his horse as the two attempted to rescue Mamie, as she continued to scream for help. As they approached the wagon Marshall McCoy could see a large amount of dynamite the wagon was carrying that was still partially hiding under the hay. The fire at the back of the wagon was fast approaching the dynamite and he knew that as soon as it reached the dynamite in the wagon that all that was in it or around it would be blown to smithereens! He knew they needed to move fast, and he pointed out the impending danger to Braveman.

The two heroes rode alongside the wagon at full speed with their trusted horses. Braveman and his horse, Bear, pulled very near to the wagon, then Braveman climbed on Bear's back balancing carefully, and then jumped off Bears back and onto the flaming wagon.

He went quickly over to Mamie and began to untie her, and he told her, "We are your true friends, and we are here to help you!"

She nodded in agreement showing great thankfulness in her eyes that she was being rescued. He quickly finished untying her as Marshall McCoy on his horse Buddy rode very close to the wagon so when she was set free, she could then get on the back of his horse and escape the burning wagon.

He told her, “Okay let’s get you out of here!”

She replied, “I can’t stand up and walk like you.” Then she pulled the blanket back that had been covering her fin.

Braveman jumped back in amazement and said “The legend is true! You’re a mermaid! Daughter of the Lake King of the Mountain Kingdom!”

Marshall McCoy looked at her single fin in amazement as well, then suddenly notice that the wagon was quickly approaching a skinning ridge with a giant cliff on one side and “Lake Mamie” on the other and the ridge was not wide enough for both the wagon and Buddy and Bear to continue riding next to it.

He shouted to Braveman, “You need to hurry!” as he pointed to the ridge.

Braveman then quickly scooped up Mamie and placed her sideways on the back of Marshall McCoy’s horse Buddy. Once she was securely holding on to him, he and Buddy rode away from the wagon and started to slow down and to get safely away from the flaming wagon. Braveman then called his horse Bear to follow Marshall McCoy to safety, so Bear rode away from the flaming wagon as well.

Braveman realizing his time was short before the wagon exploded and additionally the wagon had now reached the narrow ridge with the cliff on one side and the lake on the other knew he must free the horses pulling the wagon before the wagon exploded! He then swiftly jumped up to the front of the wagon and attempted to free the horse from the wagon, but he had no success releasing the metal bolt that secured the horse harness to the wagon. Then he quickly climbed under the harness hanging upside down, holding on with his legs and one hand as his other hand struggled to release the metal bolt. The fire was growing bigger, and the dynamite was about to explode! He knew he had just seconds before he and the wagon were blown to smithereens!

With his last possible attempt, finally, he was able to release the bolt as the horses broke free from the burning wagon a went full speed ahead to gain distance from the now slowing wagon. Braveman quickly climbed back to the top of the wagon and onto the bench as Marshall McCoy and Mamie watched from a safe distance as the fire had now reached the dynamite. He dove off the top of the wagon and into "Lake Mamie" that was to his right and as soon as he hit the safety of the water the dynamite exploded into a huge fireball that could be seen from all areas of the Mountain Lake Kingdom and sending pieces of the wagon flying in all directions!

The massive explosion made a huge hole in the ridge and breached "Lake Mamie." It was all quiet at first, then water from the lake started to rush out through the massive hole on the ridge and then began running down the giant cliff. The rushing water started forming a breathtaking majestic waterfall that was spilling into another crystal-blue lake hundreds of feet below.

Chapter 13

Meanwhile, Braverman's twelve warriors had successfully put out the raging campfires that Slick and his gang had started, and they were now gathering their horses to go join Marshall McCoy, Braveman, and Mamie at the newly formed beautiful waterfall. In the meantime, on the other side of the lake, Slick, Jimbo, and Derby were running for their lives trying to escape Marshall McCoy and his posse that they thought were chasing them. What they did not realize was that they were heading straight into very strong and fierce wild animals that were intent on rescuing Mamie and punishing the gang of convicts.

The Eagle was the first to spot the unholy trio and screeched out what seemed to echo over the whole Kingdom, as the mighty Eagle circled over the panicked escaping convicts and alerting the animals in the Kingdom to their location. The animals in the Kingdom stalked the gang like an army of warriors forming a virtual wall of wildlife with land animals and wild birds from every corner of the Mountain Lake Kingdom. When this army of animals came over the ridge and could finally see Slick and his gang, the line of bears who were in the front let out a ground-shaking roar signaling the attack was on and stopping the gang in their tracks making their knees tremble in fear. The fastest of the land animals, the wolves, coyotes, and foxes started running at the gang, followed by the ferocious badgers, bucks, and bears.

Slick and his gang started running in the other direction now away from the ferocious charging mountain animal army but right back towards Marshall McCoy and his posse. The wild birds were the first to reach the gang and started their dive booming missions with precision by striking the convicts backsides with their sharp becks and causing the gang to jump in pain after every strike, causing the gang to run faster right down towards the awaiting posse.

As Slick and his gang continued running down the ridge and now reached a clearing where Braveman, the warriors, Marshall McCoy, and Mamie all watched this amazing scene unfold in front of them as the wild birds continued their dive booming missions, and the land animals were chasing the gang down the ridge right towards them.

Mamie said, “It’s my father’s animal kingdom! They’re

here to help us and capture those bad men!"

When Slick and his gang reached the posse, they dove at the feet of Buddy and Marshall McCoy and begged them for help.

"Please help us! They are going to eat us alive! Please takes us back to jail!"

Then, Mamie yelled out and raised her hand towards the animal kingdom to stop the attack, and they immediately stopped.

Marshall McCoy said, "I'll take you back to jail, gladly!"

Then he got down off his horse Buddy and put iron handcuffs on each of the convicts so they could not get away.

He went on to say, "I'll take you back to jail alright, but this time you are going to a special federal prison where you want to be able to escape ever again! This prison is saved for only the worst of the worst convicts like you three. It has massive cement walls and is surrounded by a huge water pit full of alligators. You will never be able to bring trouble to this Mountain Lake Kingdom or the Human Kingdom ever again!"

Chapter 14

After the gang was captured, everyone assembled at the King's Lake, George and Mary celebrated the return of Mamie with a huge party. All the animals in the Kingdom were there as well as Marshall McCoy, Braveman, and his warriors. The King thanked everyone greatly for returning his lost daughter and then he requested a new peace covenant be made between the Human Kingdom and the Mountain Lake Kingdom.

The King said, "From this day forward, humans will always be welcome to the Mountain Lake Kingdom if they show care for the animals, the beautiful forest, and the majestic crystal-blue lakes within the Kingdom."

As a sign of this peace covenant the King ordered a rainbow to be placed over the waterfall in the Human Kingdom and the Mountain Lake Kingdom as a symbol of peace between them.

Then the King turned towards Mamie and gave her a sparkly beautiful ring from the royal treasure. She was so thrilled because she finally could wear some of the royal jewelry. Mary on the other hand looked a little sad and confused as to why Mamie was given a royal ring and she was not. After all, she was the one who listened and obeyed her father, and she did not leave the Kingdom but stayed by his side the whole time.

The King noticed Mary's confusion and said to her, "I have a special royal ring for you as well," and then he handed her a sparkly royal ring and she quickly put it on her finger, and she looked down and saw how beautiful it was.

The King thanked her very much for helping him and loyally staying by his side the whole time. The King went on to order additionally, a new lake to be given to the twin sisters to share. It was the lake with the new, majestic waterfall that flowed from "Lake Mamie" from the wagon explosion. This lake would be called "Twin Lakes" and it was a gift from the King because of the great joy and happiness he had that his lost daughter had been found and his family was now restored. The twin mermaid daughters were so happy and content and loved their father now more than ever. Then all the animals in the kingdom cried out and rejoiced at the news, and the celebration of the new peace covenant and the King's family restoration went far into the night.

From that moment on, there was great peace between the Human Kingdom and the Mountain Lake Kingdom, and they all lived happily ever after in peace and joy…

The End

I hope you enjoyed this story with a new twist of the "Prodigal Son!" This book is the first in a series of short fictional allegories I plan to write for families to enjoy. My goal is to have your family immersed in creative fiction that can be read in an hour to an hour and a half timeframe. Using this format, I strive to bring families closer together by spending quality time with one another around an inviting fireplace or a campfire with a cup of hot cocoa reading and listing to these stories. It is peaceful environments such as these, that allow our imaginations and dreams to overtake our current surroundings. This euphoric environment also enables the values and the "moral of the story" to be absorbed and consumed. Hopefully, in the process providing enjoyable family entertainment with powerful messages for both adults and children, and at the same time offering a family-inclusive interactive activity.

Thank you for your time and consideration in reading my book and I hope you'll have some time to visit the real crystal-blue lakes in the Eastern Sierras, like Lake Mary, Mamie, and Twin and experience your own family adventure and create lasting memories. Just remember to heed the King's instructions, "show care for the animals, the beautiful forest, and the majestic crystal-blue lakes." We need to protect these magnificent places for generations to come.

I hope you were entertained, immersed, and inspired!

S. McCoy